BREAK OUT!

Adapted by Cordelia Evans

Illustrated by Andy Bialk

Ready-to-Read

Simon Spotlight

New York   London   Toronto   Sydney   New Delhi

SIMON SPOTLIGHT
An imprint of Simon & Schuster Children's Publishing Division
1230 Avenue of the Americas, New York, New York 10020
This Simon Spotlight edition June 2017
The Emoji Movie © 2017 Sony Pictures Animation Inc. All Rights Reserved.
emoji® is a registered trademark of emoji company GmbH used under license.
For information about special discounts for bulk purchases, please contact Simon & Schuster Special Sales at
1-866-506-1949 or business@simonandschuster.com.
Manufactured in the United States of America 0517 LAK
10 9 8 7 6 5 4 3 2 1
ISBN 978-1-5344-0054-2 (hc)
ISBN 978-1-5344-0053-5 (pbk)
ISBN 978-1-5344-0055-9 (eBook)

Hi. I'm Jailbreak.
I'm an Emoji.
I'm pretty happy to be one,
but I wasn't always.

You see, my name wasn't always Jailbreak.

It used to be Linda. Linda was a princess Emoji in Textopolis. You might think being a princess is all fun and games, but it's not.

Princesses have to look pretty
and wear shiny crowns.
I didn't like being told what to do.
I wanted to look the way
I wanted to look.

One day I showed up
looking like this.
Everyone freaked out.

"If you don't change back,
I'll have you deleted!" Smiler said.

But I couldn't change back.
I'm not a pretty princess!

I wanted to live in a place
where I could have an apartment,
express myself,
and get a cat.
I wanted to live on the Cloud.

But when I tried to get there, the firewall kept me out. The firewall remembers your face, and it only lets you guess the password once.

To get past the firewall,
I needed to override its program.
So I taught myself how to code.
I became a computer programmer.

Then I met Gene and Hi-5.
Gene needed my help.
He wanted me to reprogram him.
Gene was supposed to
be only a Meh Emoji,
but he was also so much more.

"Can you do a smiley face?" I asked.
Gene smiled perfectly!
"Sleepy face?"
Gene looked sleepy!
"Shocked? Kooky?
Show me the money?"
Gene could do them all.
He wasn't like any other Emoji.
He was like magic!

I needed a special tool
to reprogram Gene,
but that tool was in the Cloud
behind the firewall.
Since Gene could make tons
of different faces, we'd have
lots of chances to guess
the firewall password.
"Listen, I'm going to help you,"
I told Gene.
"But it's not going to be easy."

I was right.
We had to run from
Anti-Virus Bots that
wanted to delete Gene.
At one point my beanie fell off.

"You're the princess!" Gene said.
"Is it true that
when a princess whistles,
birds fly down from the skies
and land on her shoulder?"

"No, that's ridiculous," I told him.
"That's a complete and total myth."

Together we explored the phone.
We went through many apps,
and even through the trash.
Finally we made it to the firewall.
But none of the passwords worked.
"You can do it, Gene," I said.
Gene guessed one last time.
Access granted!

We made it to the Cloud.
I couldn't believe it.
My dream came true.

But Gene surprised me. "Jailbreak, you're the coolest Emoji I've ever met, and after all the adventures we've had, I'm not sure I want that all to go away. I could stay here with you. Forever," Gene said.

I liked being Gene's friend,
but I needed to live in a place
where I could express myself.
"I'm not looking for a prince,"
I told Gene.

Gene was so sad that he didn't need to be reprogrammed anymore. He was naturally "meh" now. He walked off the Cloud . . . and into the clutches of a Superbot!

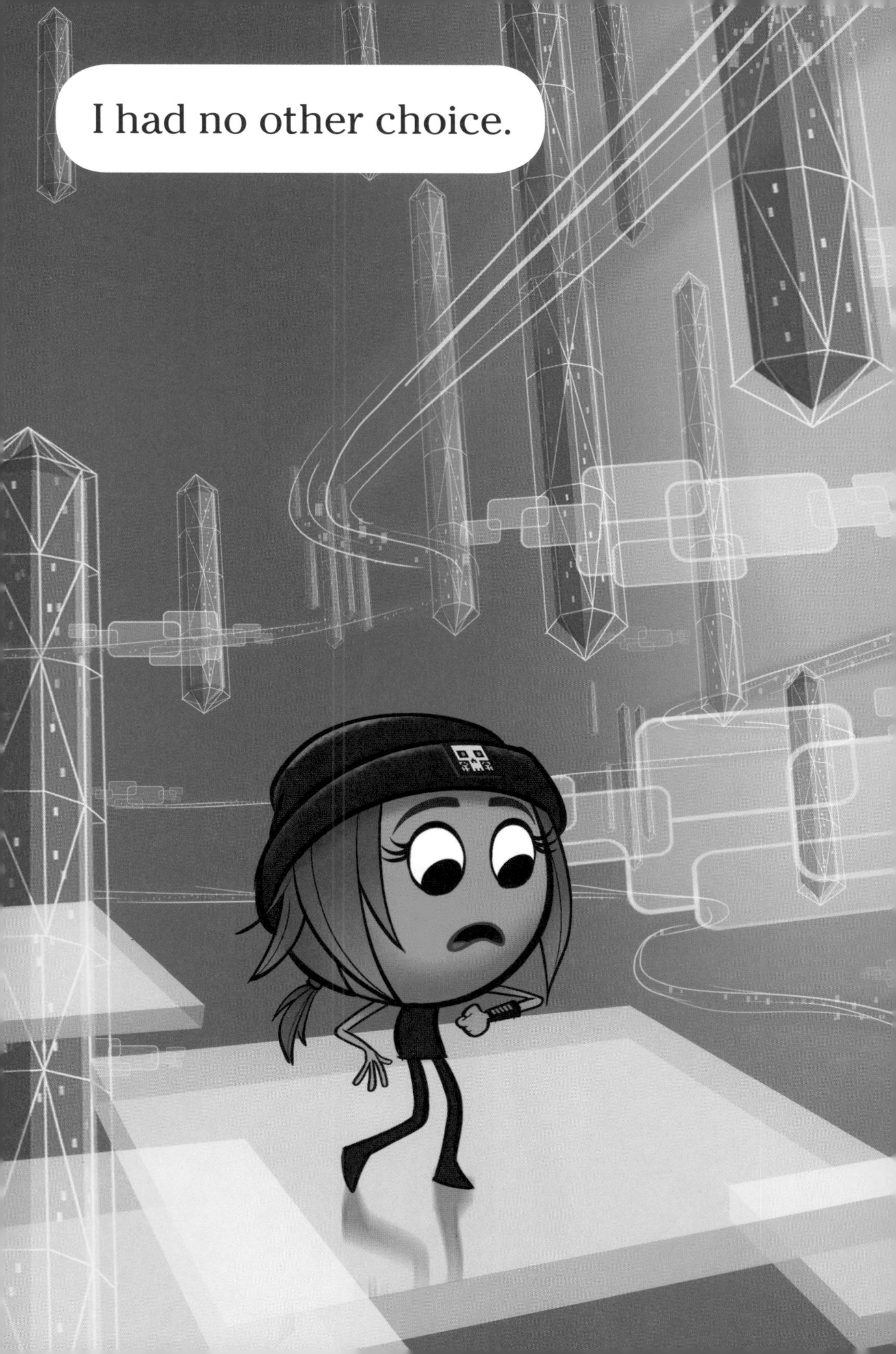
I had no other choice.

I pulled off my beanie,
puckered my lips,
and whistled a happy tune.

You see, I didn't tell
the whole story to Gene.
I'm not proud of it, but
princesses *can* call for birds.
I didn't want to do it,
but I had to save my friend.

Just as the Superbot was
about to delete Gene,
I broke in and shut it down.

Gene was saved!
But the rest of the Emojis were in trouble.
The owner of the phone, Alex, was considering wiping his data.

"I'll take it from here," Gene said. It was a risky move, but Gene showed Alex just how important it is to express yourself.

Everyone cheered.
The phone was saved!
Together we proved to the other
Emojis that there is nothing wrong
with being exactly who you are.

So now I'm back home in Textopolis, but it's cool.

You want to know why?

I'm the announcer!
I get to announce which Emoji
will be chosen next,
and I get to wear whatever I want.
Don't tell anyone I said this,
but it might even be better
than living on the Cloud.
How's that for expressing yourself?